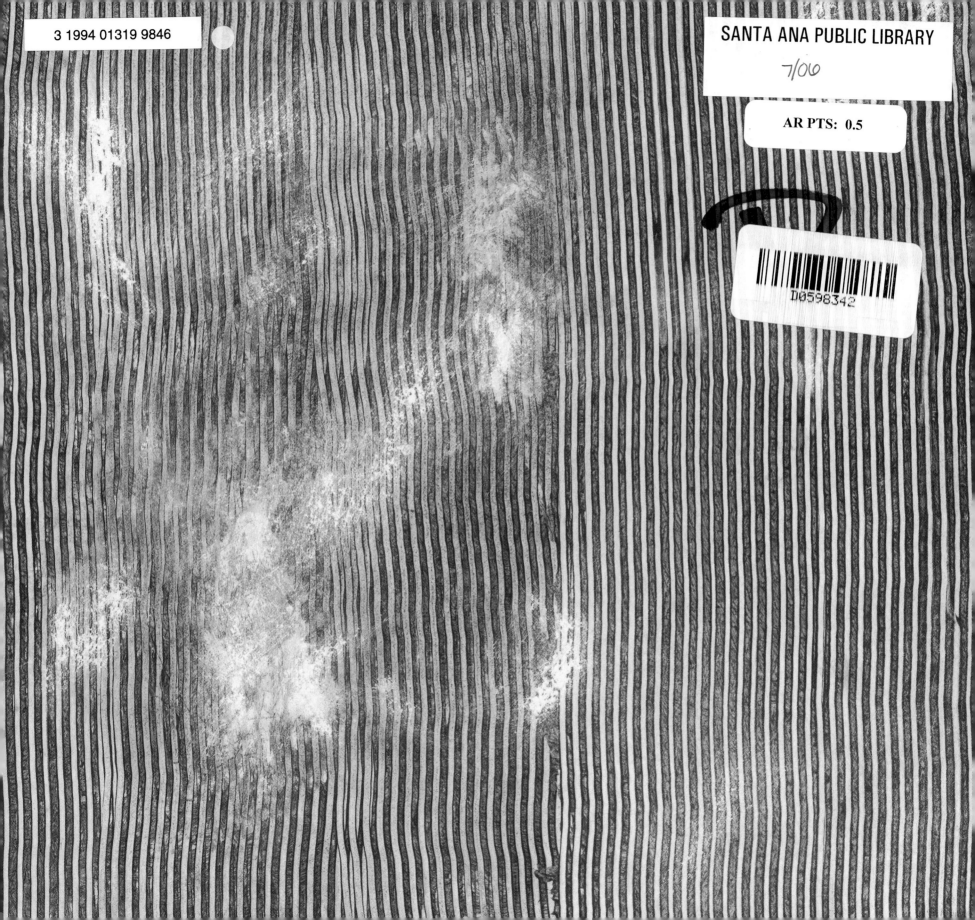

3 1994 01319 9846

SANTA ANA PUBLIC LIBRARY

7/06

AR PTS: 0.5

D0598342

Published by
PEACHTREE PUBLISHERS
1700 Chattahoochee Avenue
Atlanta, Georgia 30318-2112

www.peachtree-online.com

Text © 2006 by Tony Crunk
Illustrations © 2006 by Michael Austin

All rights reserved. No part of this publication may be reproduced, stored in a
retrieval system, or transmitted in any form or by any means—electronic,
mechanical, photocopy, recording, or any other—except for brief quotations in
printed reviews, without the prior permission of the publisher.

Art direction by Loraine M. Joyner
Typesetting by Melanie McMahon Ives

Illustrations created in acrylic on Strathmore Series 500 illustration board.

Printed in Singapore
10 9 8 7 6 5 4 3 2 1
First Edition

Library of Congress Cataloging-in-Publication Data

Crunk, Tony.
   Railroad John and the Red Rock run / written by Tony Crunk ; illustrated by
Michael Austin.-- 1st ed.
      p. cm.
   Summary: Lonesome Bob and Granny Apple Fritter have to get to Red Rock by
two o'clock or Lonesome will miss his wedding, but Railroad John has never been
late so nothing will keep him from pulling the train in by 1:59.
   ISBN 1-56145-363-3
   [1. Railroads--Trains--Fiction. 2. Weddings--Fiction. 3. West (U.S.)--Fiction. 4.
Tall tales.] I. Austin, Michael, 1965- ill. II. Title.
   PZ7.C88955Rai 2006
   [E]--dc22
                                    2005026705

For Petticoat Bill, with love and thanks
—*T. C.*

To Mom and Dennis for the trunk of old photos and the
loads of crazy family stories that go with them.
And, as always, a special thank you to Kim,
for her patience and support.
—*M. A.*

Railroad John and the Red Rock Run

Story by Tony Crunk

Pictures by Michael Austin

J PICT BK CRUNK, T.
Crunk, Tony
Railroad John and the Red
    Rock Run

                           $16.95
CENTRAL   31994013199846

Ω
PEACHTREE
ATLANTA

The Sagebrush Flyer came roaring down Coyote Pass, whistled twice, and pulled into the Sugar City station. There on the platform stood Lonesome Bob and Granny Apple Fritter.

"Howdy, Granny!" said Railroad John. "Howdy, Lonesome! Where you off to, all dressed up?"

"Lonesome aims to get hitched today," said Granny Apple Fritter. "The wedding's in Red Rock at two o'clock, and we can't be a minute late!"

"Well, it's a mighty fine day for marrying!" said Railroad John. "The Flyer hits Red Rock at exactly 1:59. I've driven this train for forty years, and we've never been late once yet!"

"Who's the lucky lady?" asked Railroad John.

"I aim to marry Wildcat Annie," said Lonesome Bob. "She's wild as a panther, but sweet as a honeybee's gold tooth."

Then he picked up his guitar-box and plucked himself out a tune:

> Oh, I been lonesome all my life,
> But I'll nevermore lonesome be.
> For I'm headin' to Red Rock to meet my bride.
> Wildcat Annie's the girl for me.

"You're a good boy, Lonesome," said Granny Apple Fritter.

The Sagebrush Flyer highballed it down the tracks, lickety-whoop and whoopety-lick. They roared around Dead Man's Curve and—

Whoa! Railroad John slammed on the brakes.

Smack-dab in the middle of the tracks sat Bad Bill, the vilest, orneriest outlaw that ever scuffed up dust. He was sitting aback Flame, his famous fire-breathing palomino, and they were both looking testy as scorpions with the prickly heat.

"Now, Railroad John, I don't mean you no harm," Bad Bill said. "But poor Flame here is plum out of grub, and he don't have much fire left in him. Show 'em, Flame."

Flame let go a huff and a puff. Bad Bill was right—it wasn't enough spark to kindle dry straw.

"Flame needs him some fire-stoking vittles," said Bad Bill. "So we'll be obliged to take that coal you're carrying."

Bad Bill and his outlaw gang loaded up twenty-seven tow sacks of Railroad John's coal and hightailed it off.

There sat the Sagebrush Flyer, chugging its last chug, and not a pebble of coal left. "Well, this is a vexation," said Railroad John.

"Now, don't you worry, Railroad!" said Granny Apple Fritter. "Look-ey here what I've got!"

It was a heaping platter of Granny's special Hard-Shell Chili-Pepper Corn-Pone Muffins that she'd baked for the wedding feast.

The Sagebrush Flyer went calahooting down the tracks, mickety-tuck and tuckety-mick, blowing steam so peppery hot it made the crows' eyes water thirty-two miles away!

On they flew, through Cayuse Canyon and Vulture's Gap. Then, just around Horseshoe Bend they ran bang-straight into the fiercest rainstorm that ever was! Thunder rolled out like cannon shot and lightning bullwhipped fire across the sky. The rain was so thick you could float toads on it.

The Sagebrush Flyer roared out over Eagle's Draw, down toward Cripplesome Creek, and—

Whoa! Up ahead, the bridge was washed clean away!

But the Sagebrush Flyer just kept on flying. The tracks were too slick for them to stop!

Lonesome Bob thought fast. He unhooked four of his guitar-box strings and lashed them together for a lariat.

CR-R-RACK!! Another lightning bolt ripped through the clouds.

Lonesome Bob lassoed the forked end and whipped it down over the creek—just in time! The Sagebrush Flyer sailed right across!

Railroad John looked at his watch. "Twenty-two minutes behind," he said. "But we're coming into Sulfur Flats. We'll make that time up now! I've driven this train for forty years, and we've never been late once yet!"

But just then the Sagebrush Flyer blurped out a cough and a wheeze and a splurt and putt-putt-puttered to a stop.

They'd used up the last of Granny's Hard-Shell Chili-Pepper Corn-Pone Muffins. There they sat, flim-flum in the middle of Sulfur Flats without a crumb of fuel left.

Lonesome Bob was in a state. He was squeezing out tears the size of elephant's eggs. He picked up his guitar-box and plucked himself out a tune:

> *Oh, I'll never make it to Red Rock on time,*
> *Wildcat Annie I'll nevermore see.*
> *Oh, I been lonesome all my life,*
> *And now I'll evermore lonesome be.*

"Times is hard all over," said Granny Apple Fritter.

But that wasn't the end of their troubles. The weather was going from rough to rocky, and now the wind was whipping up ugly and mean.

They looked out, and a cloud of feathers came flying past—
then they saw the chickens!
A clump of needles came flying by—
then they saw the porcupine!
A slosh of milk came flying by—
then they saw the cow!

Then, over the hill, bearing straight down on them, came a sure enough Idaho spine-twiner!

"Great jumpin' johnnycakes!" cried Railroad John. "Hold onto your boots! We're in for a blow!"

Here came the whirly-wind, swirling and twirling, looping and swooping. It scooped up the Sagebrush Flyer and spun it away, out across Sulfur Flats—twirling and swirling, around and around.

"Whoo-hoo!" cried Railroad John.

"Whoo-hoo!" cried Lonesome Bob and Granny Apple Fritter.

Then, just as fast as it started, the whole thing was over. That whirly-wind gave them one last swirl and set them down, train and all, gentle as a baby bundle—right gum-dab in front of the Red Rock station!

Railroad John let out a whoop. "1:59 exactly! Yes, I've driven this train for forty years, and we've never been late once yet!"

"Let's skeee-daddle," said Lonesome Bob. "Wildcat Annie's a-waiting for me!"

So Railroad John, Lonesome Bob, and Granny Apple Fritter vamoosed down to the Red Rock chapel. And there, waiting for them, was…

…nary a soul!

"Well, it's not quite two o'clock," said Granny.
But Lonesome Bob was looking solemn as cold mush.

The clock ticked off 2:00.

Then 2:01.

Then 2:02.

"That's all she wrote," said Lonesome Bob. "Looks like there won't be any marrying after all."

But just then they heard a rootin' and a tootin', a shootin' and a hootin'. Thundering up over the hill came Wildcat Annie, along with Grampa Crusty Huckabuck and a whole passel of other folks.

Wildcat Annie roared up like a dust storm riding an avalanche.

"Yee-ee-haw-w!" she whooped. "Howdy, Lonesome! Sorry I'm running a mite behind. These here outlaw varmints tried to get feisty with us, and we had to jerk a knot in their hindquarters." It was Bad Bill and his gang!

"I believe this belongs to the Sagebrush Flyer," Annie said, handing Railroad John twenty-seven tow sacks full of coal. "And look-ey what I baked for you, Granny!" It was a heaping platter of Hard-Shell Chili-Pepper Corn-Pone Muffins. "I know how much you love 'em."

"You're a good girl, Wildcat," said Granny Apple Fritter.

"Yee-ee-haw-w!" hollered the bride. "Now then! I thought there was to be a marrying here today!"

She handed Lonesome Bob his wedding present—a brand new set of guitar-box strings. Then she picked up her banjo-box and plucked herself out a tune:

> *Oh, I been a wildcat all my life,*
> *And I'll ever a wildcat be.*
> *But I'll nevermore wildcat all alone,*
> *Lonesome Bob's the boy for me.*

So Wildcat Annie and Lonesome Bob were married that afternoon.

And my, oh my, you never saw such a wedding! There was singing and dancing, hooting and hollering, jack-a-naping and rusty-cutting. Why, Granny Apple Fritter and Grampa Crusty Huckabuck even did a little courting and sparking themselves!

And Railroad John stayed fourteen minutes later than he should have. But he wasn't worried at all—he knew he'd make his next stop on time.

"I've driven this train for forty years," he said, "and we've never been late once yet!"

Granny Apple Fritter's Hard-Shell Chili-Pepper Corn Pone Muffins

Ingredients:

1 cup cactus flour

2 cups Meadow Maid ® brand Hard-Shell Corn Meal (with patented

   Triple-X Baking Power!)

2 porcupine eggs, lightly beaten

1/2 cup rattlesnake milk

1 teaspoon pure dragon's tooth extract

1/2 cup lightning-roasted hot chili peppers, diced

Directions:

Preheat oven to 1250 degrees.

Sift together flour and meal.

In a separate bowl, mix eggs, milk, and extract.

Stir egg mixture into dry ingredients.

Fold in diced peppers.

Pour into lightly greased #12 iron muffin tin.

Bake 45 to 50 minutes, or until crazy hot.

Serve cautiously.

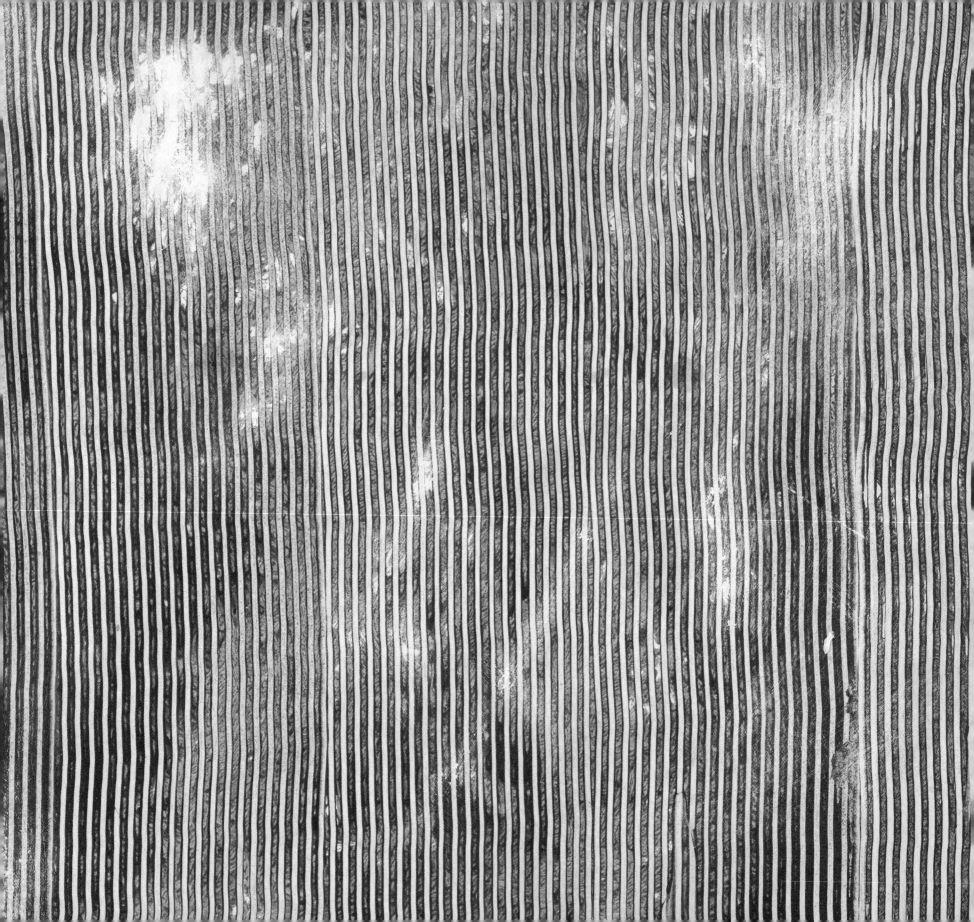